Latkes for Santa Claus

WRITTEN BY
Janie Emaus

Sky Pony Press
New York

ILLUSTRATED BY
Bryan Langdo

Sky Pony Press books may be purchased in bulk at special discounts for sales promotion, corporate gifts, fund-raising, or educational purposes. Special editions can also be created to specifications. For details, contact the Special Sales Department, Sky Pony Press, 307 West 36th Street, 11th Floor, New York, NY 10018 or info@skyhorsepublishing.com.

Sky Pony® is a registered trademark of Skyhorse Publishing, Inc.®, a Delaware corporation.

Visit our website at www.skyponypress.com.

10 9 8 7 6 5 4 3 2 1

Manufactured in China, July 2020
This product conforms to CPSIA 2008

Library of Congress Cataloging-in-Publication Data is available on file.

Cover design by Daniel Brount
Cover illustration by Bryan Langdo

Print ISBN: 978-1-5107-5988-6
Ebook ISBN: 978-1-5107-5989-3

For my husband, Rick, who brings out the best in me. —JE

For my kids, Oliver and Harper. —BL

To: Santa@thenorthpole.com

From: Anna@myhouse.com

My new dad and stepbrother celebrate Christmas, so you're coming to my house for the very first time. And I think you must be REALLY tired of cookies. I'm going to leave you the best Santa treat ever.

Anna

"Santa is too busy to answer emails." Michael sat on the floor spinning Anna's dreidel. "Besides, *my* cookies are the best Santa treat *ever*."

He launched the dreidel across the floor.

Anna's mind whirled.

"Ready to bake?" Michael asked.

Anna knew she could think of something better than cookies.

A pot of matzo ball soup simmered on the stove. Steam swirled toward Anna like chimney smoke. The chickeny smell made her stomach growl.

"Yes!" She pumped her fist. "I'll bet Santa would love Bubbe Sadie's matzo ball soup."

"Santa can't eat soup with his fingers," Michael said. "Besides, Santa loves *my* sugar cookies."

She imagined—

Balls of matzo zooming by.

Santa *gulping* on his sled.

Slurp. Burb. Slop. Spill.

Matzo balls on Santa's head.

Anna sighed. Michael was right. Matzo ball soup would never do.

Anna peeked into a pan of Aunt Bea's noodle kugel.

"Yes!" She clapped her hands. "I'll bet Santa would love the sweet taste of noodle kugel."

"The noodles look like worms," Michael said. "And Santa can't eat kugel with his fingers."

He measured flour into a bowl.

"Besides, Santa loves *my* oatmeal cookies."

Anna imagined—

Chunks of kugel zipping by.

Santa *munching* on his sled.

Slurp. Burp. Slop. Spill.

Noodle kugel on his head.

Anna sighed. Michael was right. Noodle kugel would never do.

Anna opened a jar of Aunt Sarah's tzimmes.

"Yes! I'll bet Santa will love this stew."

"Squishy carrots and raisins?" Michael rolled his eyes. "Santa can't eat stew with his fingers. Besides, Santa loves *my* chocolate chip cookies."

Anna imagined—

A bowl of stew zipping by.

Santa *spooning* on his sled.

Slurp. Burp. Slop. Spill.

Gobs of stew on Santa's head.

Anna sighed. Michael was right. Tzimmes would never do.

She needed something Santa could eat with his fingers that wouldn't make a mess.

She snuck away and sat down in her thinking spot.

Her mind spun like a dizzy dreidel. . . .

Until, finally, it landed on exactly what she was looking for.

Round, just like a cookie.

But it wasn't a cookie.

No spills. No slurps. (Well, maybe a burp.)

Her mother had been frying them all afternoon. She found them wrapped up in the fridge and hid a plateful in the pantry.

That night, Anna lay in bed with her eyes
wide open. Through her bedroom window, she
watched the icy wind lift her snowman's scarf
and carry it across the yard like a magic carpet.

Everyone in the house fell asleep. Everyone but Anna.

She tiptoed into the pantry. She added four of her treats to the plate of Michael's cookies.

Latkes!

Yes! Latkes were perfect.

Anna imagined—

A latke in Santa's hand.

Latkes in the sled.

Latkes in his tummy

as she hurried off to bed.

The wind whistled Christmas songs.
The stars twinkled like Hanukkah lights.

Any minute now, Santa's reindeer would *click, clack* on the roof.
She closed her eyes for a teensy tiny bit.

"It's Christmas!" Michael shouted, startling Anna.

She jumped out of bed and they scrambled into the living room.

"My cookies are all gone!" Michael whooped.

"So are my latkes!" Anna danced around.

Michael frowned at her. "You gave him latkes?"

"They are perfect to eat with your fingers." Anna wiggled her fingers in Michael's face.

Just then, the computer dinged, signaling a new email.

To: Anna@myhouse.com

From: Santa@thenorthpole.com

I loved your latkes. So did Mrs. Claus. Can you please send her the recipe to add to her cookbook? I can't wait to see what special treat you leave me next year!

Santa

"He answered?" Michael leaned over Anna's shoulder. "I guess, cookies *are* kind of boring. How about next year, we leave Grandma Linda's lemon jello?"

"Santa can't eat jello with his fingers," Anna teased.

"How about latke brownies?" Michael asked.

"Hmmm." Anna pressed her finger to her lips. "I bet together we can think of something really special. We have lots of time to figure it out!"

Recipes from
When Santa's Stomach Grumbles
by Mrs. Claus

Grandma Sylvia's Potato Latkes

This recipe makes 20 latkes, enough for Santa, Mrs. Claus, and all the reindeer.

Ingredients	**Utensils**
4 large potatoes	Vegetable peeler
1 onion	Knife
2 eggs	Large bowl
3 tablespoons flour	Food processor
Salt	Whisk/fork
Pepper	Frying pan
Oil for the pan	Cookie sheets
	Paper towels

Instructions

1. Use the vegetable peeler to peel the skin off the potatoes.

2. Have an adult help you cut the potatoes into chunks about 1 inch in size.

3. Fill a bowl with cold water.

4. Put the potatoes in the water. This will keep them from turning brown.

5. With your adult's help, place the cut potatoes in a food processor and chop them up.

6. Cut the onion in 1-inch pieces. If the onion makes you cry, don't worry. Cutting onions makes everyone cry, even Mrs. Claus.

7. With the help of your adult, chop the onions in the food processor.

8. Mix the onions and potatoes together.

9. Whisk the eggs.

10. Add the eggs to the onion and potato mixture.

11. Add the flour. This will make everything stick together.

12. Add a pinch of salt and a pinch of pepper. A pinch is a small amount held between your thumb and forefinger.

13. Pour about ¼ inch of oil into the frying pan.

14. Heat the oil.

15. With your adult's help, drop 1 tablespoon of mixture into the hot oil. BE VERY CAREFUL.

16. Fry until the latke is crisp and golden brown.

17. Turn it over and fry on the other side.

18. Remove latke and place on a paper towel–lined cookie sheet to remove excess grease and cool.

19. Repeat until all the mixture is fried.

20. Serve with applesauce or sour cream or both.

21. Have lots of fun eating your latkes!

Santa's Sprinkled Sugary Shapes

This recipe makes about 36 cookies.

Ingredients

⅔ cup shortening

¾ cup granulated sugar

1 teaspoon vanilla

1 egg

4 teaspoons milk

¼ teaspoon salt

2 cups flour

1½ teaspoon baking powder

Assorted sprinkles

Utensils

Large mixing bowl

Electric mixer

Mixing spoon

Small bowl

Measuring spoons

Measuring cups

Rolling pin

Cookie-cutter shapes: Santa Claus, Trees, Stars, Snowmen, Reindeer

Cookie sheet

Wire rack

Instructions

Make your dough.

1. Mix shortening, sugar, and vanilla. Use your electric mixer on medium speed.

2. Add egg. Beat until light and fluffy.

3. Stir in milk.

4. In a small bowl, mix together the salt, flour, and baking powder.

5. Add this mixture to the large mixing bowl.

6. Blend into a creamy mixture.

7. You now have the dough for making your cookies.

8. Divide into two big balls and put back into the bowl.

9. Place bowl in the refrigerator to get cold.

10. Help your adult wash measuring spoons and cups while waiting for dough to cool.

Roll your cookies.

11. Sprinkle some flour onto a cutting board or large surface.

12. Using your rolling pin, roll out the dough until $\frac{1}{8}$ inch thick, which is about as thick as your thumb.

13. Cut dough using your cookie-cutter shapes of choice.

14. Place your shapes on an ungreased cookie sheet.

15. Bake at 375°F for 7 to 8 minutes or until edges are firm and brown.

16. Transfer to a wire rack to cool.

Decorate your cookies.

17. While cookies are still warm, sprinkle shapes with colored sugar dots.

18. Make a happy face on Santa Claus, sprinkle ornaments on the tree, give the snowmen a funny hat, or give the reindeer a silly smile.

Serve cookies with a big, tall glass of cold milk.

Yummy for your tummy!